THE HANDMADE ALPHABET

Laura Rankin

PUFFIN BOOKS

For Nick and Brendan, with love

The artist and publisher appreciate the help of
Alan Barwiolek, M.A.,
American Sign Language/Deaf Culture Consultant.

PUFFIN BOOKS
Published by the Penguin Group
Penguin Putnam Books for Young Readers,
345 Hudson Street, New York, New York 10014, U.S.A.
Penguin Books Ltd, 80 Strand, London WC2R ORL, England
Penguin Books Australia Ltd, Ringwood, Victoria, Australia
Penguin Books Canada Ltd, 10 Alcorn Avenue, Toronto, Ontario, Canada M4V 3B2
Penguin Books (N.Z.) Ltd, 182-190 Wairau Road, Auckland 10, New Zealand
Penguin Books Ltd, Registered Offices: Harmondsworth, Middlesex, England

Originally published in hardcover by Dial Books
A member of Penguin Putnam Inc.

Library of Congress Catalog Card Number: 90-24593
Manufactured in China
First Puffin Pied Piper Printing 1996
ISBN 978-0-14-055876-0
A Pied Piper Book is
a registered trademark of Dial Books,
a member of Penguin Putnam Inc.,
® TM 1,163,686 and ® TM 1,054,312.

30

The art for each picture consists of colored pencil
on charcoal paper, which is scanner-separated
and reproduced in full color.

THE HANDMADE ALPHABET

Artist's Note

My older stepson is deaf. For the first eighteen years of his life he moved with dignity yet difficulty through the hearing world, relying primarily on the complex art of lipreading for his verbal understanding. Then he went to Gallaudet University in Washington, D.C., and learned American Sign Language. As a visual language it was completely accessible to him and allowed him to share ideas fully. Through it he gained more thorough understanding and total communication.

The manual alphabet, an integral part of American Sign Language, was my first contact with signing. As an outsider to deaf culture, my abilities in this mode are limited. However, my respect is deep and it is my wish that this introduction to the alphabet begin to open the world of sign communication to all who see this book.

—LAURA RANKIN
Buffalo, New York

A

C

E

F

G

H

J

K

L

N

R

S

U

V

X

Y

The artwork on each page of this book shows a handshape for the manual alphabet and a corresponding letter of the written alphabet. Other images shown in the art are listed below:

A	Asparagus		N	Nails
B	Bubbles		O	Ornament
C	Cup		P	Paints, Palette
D	Dragonfly		Q	Quilt
E	Eraser		R	Ribbon
F	Fog		S	Stamps
G	Glove		T	Thimbles, Thread
H	Hole		U	Umbrella
I	Icicles		V	Valentine
J	Jam, Jar		W	Web
K	Keys		X	X ray
L	Lace		Y	Yo-yo
M	Mirror		Z	Zipper

The title page shows the handshape for A; the back cover shows the handshape for D; and the front cover shows the handshapes for W, E, H, B, Y, and I.

Acknowledgments

I thank the following people for their help and support:

Everyone at St. Mary's School for the Deaf in Buffalo, New York, especially Sister Virginia Young; Sister Loretta Young; Sister Pauline LeRoy; Tiffany Anderson; Tom (T.J.) Anderson, Jr. and Tom (T.J.) Anderson, Sr.; Jennifer Bump; Norine D. Borkowski; Charlie James Clemente; Jane D'Amico; John Hencker; Bonnie Henderson; Caitlin LaLonde; Samantha Marguccio; Wendy Miller; Sandy Orlando; Lamar James Ray; and Mary Tousley, S.S.J.

Heartfelt thanks to Tony Bannon.

*My devotion I send to Aunt Barbara —
who first taught me the manual alphabet — for her love and courage.*

Finally, I thank my parents, Ed and Mary Rankin, for their love and example.